CALLING ALL HAM-HAMS!

By Michael Anthony Steele
Illustrated by Bill Alger

SCHOLASTIC INC.
New York Toronto London Auckland Sydney
Mexico City New Delhi Hong Kong Buenos Aires

ISBN 0-439-54236-7

Published by Scholastic Inc.
SCHOLASTIC and associated logos are trademarks and/or registered trademarks of Scholastic Inc.

Design by Peter Koblish

12 11 10 9 8 7 6 5 4 3 2 1 3 4 5 6 7 8/0
Printed in the U.S.A.
First printing, May 2003

THE GREAT ESCAPE

From inside his carrier, Hamtaro watched Laura Haruna walking around her bedroom. His owner was getting ready to leave.

I wish Laura would hurry up and go to school, thought Hamtaro. *I can't wait to go to the Ham-Ham clubhouse!*

"Okay, I'm going, Hamtaro!"

said Laura. "Bye!" She walked out the door.

"Time for my great escape!" Hamtaro said.

The hamster climbed out of his carrier and scurried behind the bed. He crawled through the secret hole in the wall. Then he ran along the roof and slid down the drainpipe.

On the ground, Hamtaro ran past Brandy, Laura's dog. "*Hamha*, Brandy!" he said, saying hello.

Brandy yawned. She was always sleeping.

Hamtaro scampered to Oak Tree

"I tripped on a big blade of grass," cried Oxnard, "and it slipped out of my paws!"

"We've all lost sunflower seeds," said Boss. "You'll find another one before you know it."

"How can you be sure?" Oxnard asked sadly. "I may never get another seed again!"

Hamtaro wanted to make Oxnard happy again. They had to find his sunflower seed!

POT LUCK!

Hamtaro peered closer. Oxnard was sitting on something. "Wait a second," said Hamtaro. "Move over."

Oxnard moved over and there was his sunflower seed. He had been sitting on it.

"Hamtaro, you're the greatest hamster in the world!" Oxnard said.

"Let's go to the clubhouse and see who's there!" said Hamtaro.

On the way there the three Ham-Hams ran into some friends.

"*Hamha!*" said Pashmina. She was wearing the pretty pink scarf she always wore.

Penelope was there too. She was such a shy young hamster that she wore a little yellow blanket over her head.

Boss stared at three Ham-Hams standing behind Pashmina and Penelope. "Who have you brought with you?" he asked.

"Some new friends," replied Pashmina.

"A hamster can never have enough friends!" said Hamtaro.

One tall Ham-Ham carried a book. "My name is Maxwell," he said. "I live in a bookstore."

Pashmina pointed to two other hamsters. "That's Panda and Sandy," she said.

Panda looked just like a panda bear.

Sandy danced, and twirled a

long ribbon. "Hi!" she chirped. "I'm Sandy!"

Just then, a big red pot jumped out of nowhere and landed in front of the hamsters. Everyone screamed.

"That pot is alive!" Boss yelled.

TO THE CLUBHOUSE!

Boss ran up to the mysterious pot. "You can't scare us, you old haunted pot!" he yelled.

Boss tried to hit the pot with his shovel. The red pot jumped out of the way. Boss raised his shovel to swing again. "This time I've got you!" he cried.

"Hold it!" Hamtaro yelled. He

sniffed all around the pot. *Hif-hif! Hif-hif!*

"Why did you stop me?" Boss asked.

"I smell a hamster!" said Hamtaro. He sniffed again. "My nose never lies."

The pot raised off the ground. A hamster wearing a cap poked his head out from underneath the pot.

"Trick or treat!" he said. "Hi, everybody! I'm Cappy!"

"*Hamha!*" everyone replied.

"Do you want to join our club?" asked Hamtaro.

"Yeah!" Cappy said. He smiled happily.

"Come on!" said Hamtaro. "We'll show you the underground clubhouse and introduce you to all the other Ham-Hams."

"This way, gang," said Boss. "Follow me!"

Boss hurried into a hole under a big tree. The other Ham-Hams followed him. They scurried down a tunnel and through the clubhouse door.

The clubhouse was where Boss

lived. It was a fun place. It had stairs to climb, chairs to sit in, and games to play.

Once inside, Hamtaro introduced the new hamsters to his other friends in the clubhouse.

"That's Dexter," said Hamtaro. He pointed to a hamster wearing a bow tie. Dexter had markings on his fur that looked like eyeglasses.

"And this guy is Howdy," said Hamtaro. He pointed to a hamster wearing a red apron.

"Howdy hodely hooah!" Howdy yelled. "Here's a new Ham-Ham song!" He began to dance and sing. *"We're the new Ham-Hams, but here's the rub, got to say 'howdy' if you want to join the club! I'm a new Ham-Ham, watch me dance, you can all see my underpants!"*

Howdy laughed at his silly song.

But he was the only one who thought it was funny.

"He's always doing something to get attention," said Dexter.

"What was that?" asked Howdy. He gave Dexter an angry look.

"Uh . . . I was just saying we should take turns cleaning," said Dexter, "because hamsters love to keep their houses tidy."

Everyone agreed.

"Hamtaro," said Maxwell, "aren't you forgetting someone?" Maxwell pointed to a hamster upstairs. The hamster was sleeping in a sock and snoring. *ZuZuZu!*

"Oh, right," said Hamtaro. "That's Snoozer. He sleeps all the time."

"Lucky guy," said Maxwell.

"Does anyone want to play a game of hide-and-seek with me?" asked Hamtaro.

"That sounds good to me," said Oxnard.

Penelope jumped up and down with glee. "*Ookwee!*" she squealed. That was the only noise she could make.

Hamtaro loved having so many new friends!

ROWDY HAM-HAMS

Tap! Tap!

Hamtaro and Maxwell watched Panda use a nut as a hammer to build a wooden desk. "Here's our official clubhouse desk," Panda said.

"Great!" said Maxwell. "Now I'll have someplace to read my favorite books."

"And it will make a really great place to hide," said Hamtaro.

"My owners are carpenters," said Panda. "I want to be a carpenter myself."

"You're already a great builder," said Hamtaro.

"A handy Ham like no other," Maxwell agreed.

In another part of the clubhouse, Howdy and Oxnard were both pulling on a toy truck.

"This is my truck and you can't play with it!" yelled Oxnard. "Get your own toy, Howdy!"

"Quit being selfish," said Howdy. "Let me have a turn!"

They pulled so hard that the truck broke into two pieces.

"You broke my new truck!" cried Oxnard.

Dexter strode over to Howdy. "This just proves that being a bully doesn't get you anywhere," he said.

"Looky here. . . ," Howdy said angrily, starting to argue.

Just then, Cappy snuck up behind Dexter. Cappy was still wearing his red pot, so Dexter was startled. He jumped back and landed on Howdy.

"Get off of me!" Howdy yelled.

Howdy began to chase Dexter around the clubhouse. They crashed into Panda's new desk and broke it. Then Howdy started chasing Dexter again.

"Look at what they did to my

desk!" cried Panda. "Hey, get back here!" He joined the chase.

Dexter, Howdy, and Panda ran up the stairs. They zoomed past Sandy.

"Cool!" said Sandy. "A hamster race!"

Pashmina jumped in front of Dexter, trying to stop the chase. "Don't fight, you guys," she said.

The running Ham-Hams did not listen. They jumped over Pashmina and tangled her scarf.

"Look at what you did to my lucky pink scarf!" yelled Pashmina. Then she joined the chase, too.

They all jumped over Snoozer, but he did not wake up. *ZuZuZu!*

Hamtaro watched them from downstairs. "Calm down, guys!" he called. "Let's not fight!"

But the Ham-Hams didn't even slow down.

NO MORE CLUBHOUSE?

Boss sat in his favorite chair. He was holding a white flower. *"A flower so soft and lovely, I have never seen,"* Boss sang. *"Secretly plucked from Bijou's garden, which is so green."* Boss had a crush on a pretty hamster named Bijou.

Suddenly, Dexter, Howdy, Panda, and Pashmina ran over Boss.

"Don't step on my nose!" Boss yelled.

But they stepped on his nose anyway. They knocked him out of his chair and crushed his flower.

"Oh no! My flower!" Boss said.

Meanwhile, Oxnard was still very upset about his broken truck. "Howdy broke my truck!" he cried.

Maxwell was upset about the broken desk. "They broke the new desk!" he yelled.

Pashmina was mad about her scarf. "You guys owe me a new scarf!" she screamed.

Hamtaro watched the Ham-Hams running around the clubhouse. He wished he could keep them from fighting.

Boss watched them too. But the Ham-Hams did not seem to care about what they broke or whose feelings they hurt.

"Enough!" Boss yelled. "Stop the madness, you monsters!"

All of the Ham-Hams stopped running and stared at Boss.

"I invited you here to play, but you are all treating my house like a jungle gym!" shouted Boss. "I can't take it anymore! Everyone out of the clubhouse!"

"Calm down," said Hamtaro. "There's no reason to get upset."

But Boss's face turned red with anger. "Just get out and leave me alone!" he yelled. He grabbed all of the Ham-Hams and threw them out of the clubhouse.

They flew through the tunnel and

landed in a big pile.

Boss slammed the clubhouse door behind them.

"I don't know what we did," said Oxnard. "But we sure made Boss mad."

"Yeah," Hamtaro agreed. "I guess we got a bit too rowdy."

"Does this mean no more visiting the clubhouse?" Dexter asked. "No more tea and sunflower seeds?"

THE PERFECT MARK

Hamtaro sat in his carrier all by himself. He did not feel like nibbling sunflower seeds. He did not want to burrow in his wood chips. He did not feel like doing anything.

The Ham-Hams are in danger of having our clubhouse broken up, he thought. *I don't want to lose all my new friends. What am I going to do?*

Laura and Kana walked into the bedroom. They had just gotten out of school. Seeing them both made Hamtaro feel a little better.

"Hi Hamtaro," said Laura and Kana.

Maybe Laura can help me figure out what to do! thought Hamtaro.

"Tell Hamtaro about your test," said Kana.

Laura reached into her backpack. She pulled out a piece of paper and held it up for Hamtaro to see.

"Ta-da!" said Laura.

The paper had some writing on

it. Hamtaro did not know what it meant.

A piece of paper? Hamtaro thought. I don't see how that will help me. But Laura is excited, so it must be good news.

"I got a perfect mark!" Laura said with a big smile.

Hamtaro was happy for Laura, but he was still worried about Boss.

How could they make it up to him? Hamtaro got on his hamster wheel. Running on his wheel helped him think. It made him feel better too.

"Look! Hamtaro's happy about my perfect mark," Laura said. "Thanks, Hamtaro!"

"I told you everyone would be glad for you," said Kana.

"I don't know why I was so worried," Laura replied. "Do you want to go play?"

"Sure!" said Kana.

"See you later, Hamtaro," Laura said.

The two girls left the bedroom.

Laura was worried about how her friends would feel, Hamtaro thought. *Doesn't she know that her friends will like her no matter what? That's what friends are for!*

Hamtaro stopped running. "That's it!" he said. "Boss is our friend. And friends like one another no matter what!"

He climbed out of his carrier. He had to talk to Boss!

OUT ON A LIMB

Boss sat inside the clubhouse all by himself. He crossed his arms over his chest and felt very grumpy. "I like it better by myself," he said. "Who needs friends anyway?"

Boss thought for a moment.

"I do!" he yelled.

Boss stood up and paced back and forth. "I can't help worrying about Hamtaro and the others," he said. "How are they going to make it on their own?"

He shook his head. "Nope, forget it, it's not my problem anymore."

Suddenly Boss heard someone snoring. *ZuZuZu!* He was not alone after all. Snoozer was asleep upstairs. The little hamster snored very loudly. Then Snoozer started to sing in his sleep.

"*Can't buy me love*," Snoozer sang. "Everybody needs somebody."

"Snoozer is right," Boss said. "I

have to get the Ham-Hams to come back."

Boss ran out of the clubhouse. He scampered through the tunnel and climbed out of the hole under the big tree.

How will I ever find them? he wondered.

Boss looked up at the big tree above him. *That's how!* he thought.

Boss climbed the tall tree. He scurried onto one of the highest branches, and carefully climbed to the tip of the long limb.

"Ham-Hams!" yelled Boss. "Please come back!"

Boss opened his mouth to shout again. Instead, he slipped and fell. He grabbed the tip of the branch with his paw.

The ground was far below him. Boss didn't know how much longer he could hold on!

CALLING ALL HAM-HAMS!

Hamtaro ran to the park. The rest of the Ham-Hams were already there.

"It looks as if we're all thinking the same thing," said Hamtaro. "Let's go and set things right!"

"How do we do that?" asked Maxwell.

"First of all, I'll apologize to Boss," said Hamtaro.

"I don't know if it's going to be that easy," said Howdy. "What if he was serious about kicking us out of the clubhouse?"

Pashmina lowered her head sadly.

"Boss can be bossy, but there's nothing to be afraid of. Boss is our friend. I'm sure he likes us as much as we like him!" said Hamtaro.

Hamtaro ran toward the big tree. "Come on!" he said.

"Somebody! Help!" a voice shouted.

"That sounded like Boss," said Pashmina.

"Help!" Boss cried.

Pashmina peered up. "Look!"

Everyone looked up and saw Boss hanging from the end of a long branch.

"Oh no! Boss is going to fall!" said Oxnard.

HAM-HAMS TO THE RESCUE!

"Help me!" yelled Boss. He kicked his paws in the air as he dangled far above the ground.

"Hang on!" Hamtaro yelled. "I'm coming!"

Hamtaro quickly climbed up the side of the tree trunk.

"Be careful, Hamtaro!" shouted the Ham-Hams.

"I have an idea!" Dexter said. He led the rest of the Ham-Hams into the bushes.

Hamtaro scurried onto the tree limb. "I'm on my way, Boss!" he called.

Hamtaro carefully crawled onto the end of the branch. He reached out to Boss. "Here," he said. "Grab my paw!"

"I'll try," said Boss.

Suddenly, the end of the tree limb snapped. Hamtaro and Boss fell. It was a long way down. They were going to hit the ground.

Dexter and the other Ham-Hams moved underneath them. They had made a giant net out of leaves and grass. They tried to get the net right under Hamtaro and Boss.

Hamtaro and Boss kept falling.

But they did not hit the ground. They landed in the net and then bounced gently.

"We're saved!" cried Hamtaro and Boss.

"Yay!" cried the Ham-Hams.

"That's what happens when we

all work together," Hamtaro said. "We saved Boss from a nasty fall!"

"Thanks, Hamtaro," Boss said. "Thanks, Ham-Hams!"

Then Hamtaro remembered what had happened at the clubhouse. "Boss, about this morning," he said. "We've got something to say to you."

"Don't get all serious on me," Boss said. "Let's go back to the clubhouse and have some fun!"

"But, Boss —" said Hamtaro.

"I really missed you guys," Boss broke in. "And anyway, you guys need me around. It's dangerous out there."

"You're right!" Hamtaro agreed.

All of the Ham-Hams cheered.

At the clubhouse, things were back to normal. Oxnard was crying because he had lost his sunflower seed again. Panda was hammering loudly. Howdy and Dexter were arguing again. And Snoozer was sleeping through all of the noise.

A HAPPY HAMTARO

That night, Laura was writing in her special notebook. It had a picture of a hamster on it that looked just like Hamtaro.

Hamtaro sat on Laura's desk and happily nibbled sunflower seeds.

"I got a perfect score on my test today," said Laura as she wrote.

I had a big day, too, Hamtaro

thought. *We were really loud and Boss made us leave. But even though he was angry, he was still our friend. In fact, all of the Ham-Hams helped Boss when he was in trouble. That's what friends are for.*

"What will tomorrow's big adventure be, Hamtaro?" said Laura.

Hamtaro did not know. What he did know was that he would always have plenty of friends to share his adventures!